WHAT GOOD IS A DRAGON?

Written & Illustrated by
Patrick Carlson

What Good Is A Dragon?

A **king** appeared before his **court** holding a **baby dragon.**

"This dragon is for the queen's birthday," the king said, "and must be delivered in time for her party."

A young man named Alexander raised his hand.

"I'll do it!"

Alexander put the
dragon
in his pack
and **left the castle.**

Alexander approached an **old bridge.** As he crossed, an **ogre** crawled from the river below.

"I must deliver this dragon to the queen for her birthday," Alexander said. "What does the **queen** need with a **dragon?**" the ogre asked.

"My walking stick is a better gift. It is sturdy and will help the queen stroll through her kingdom with ease. Give this to the queen."

Alexander took the **ogre's walking stick** and continued his journey.

Alexander crossed a **grassy field** where **a brave knight** was on patrol.

"I must deliver this **dragon** and this **walking stick** to the **queen** for her birthday," Alexander said.

"what does the **queen** need with a **dragon** and a **walking stick**?

My helmet is a better gift. With this, she can lead great armies. **Give this to the queen."**

Alexander placed the helmet on his head and carried on down the path.

The path led to a sandy beach.
Basking on a large rock, a mermaid sang.

"I am on my way to deliver a dragon, a walking stick, and a knight's helmet to the queen for her birthday," Alexander announced.

"What does the queen need with a dragon, a walking stick, and a helmet?" she asked.

"I have a magic shell from the deep. With this, she can command the creatures of the sea. Give this to her."

Alexander accepted the shell and plodded up the path to the castle.

Alexander arrived at the queen's castle. As he crossed the moat, a kraken slithered from the water.

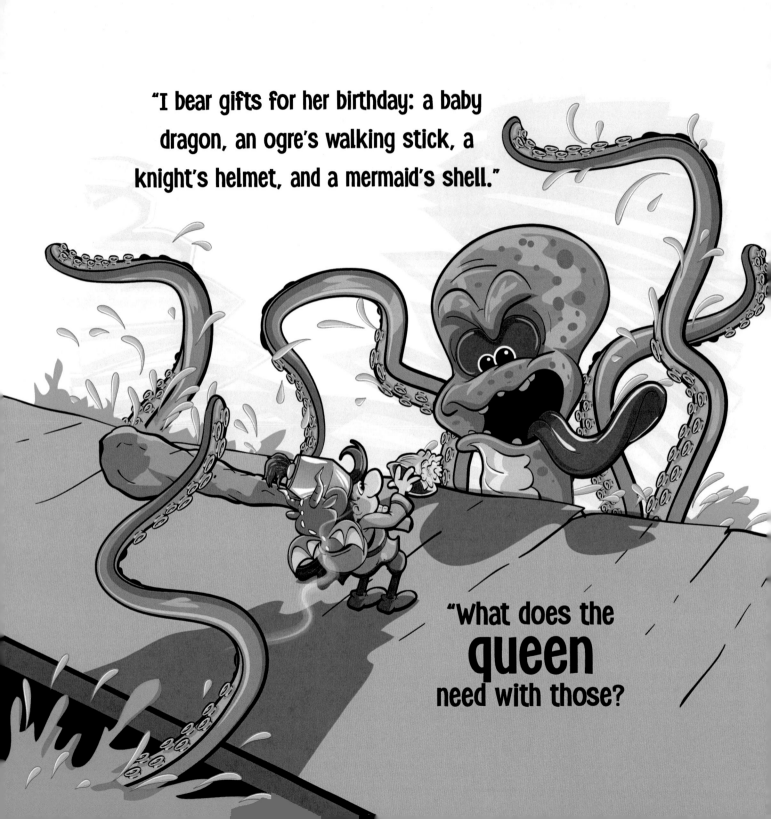

A giant pearl from the sea will make her the most beautiful queen in the world. Give this to her."

Alexander balanced the pearl on his head and tiptoed through the castle gate.

Alexander approached the throne and
laid the gifts before the queen.

The queen picked up the baby dragon, ignoring the other gifts.

"This is just what I needed!"

Alexander was confused.

"Your Highness, these other gifts grant you power and beauty. If you're not interested in them...

...what good is the
dragon?"

Made in United States
Orlando, FL
08 March 2023